MW00779435

THE SOMBER HILARITY

RITA PUSKAS

ISBN: 978-1-66787-065-6

I Hate it here...

1

The Tea Party

"I wonder what David Foster Wallace's suicide note said? I bet it was epic and probably a little confusing."

I say this to my father as he sets in front of me a coffee and carton of cream.

He rolls his eyes in a oh-Christ-not-again-kind-of-way, pauses, then says, "Maybe it said: I could not simplify myself?"

He sticks a finger into his tea to check the temperature.

"Maybe" I say clearing my throat.

"It said, done because we are too menny? M-E-N-N-Y." I look up to see if he gets the literary reference. He does, chuckles, and I can't help but smile.

My father likes to remind me that I've already out lived, Jim Morrison, Janis Joplin, Jimi Hendrix, Jesus Christ, and if I can hold out for another three years Vincent Van Gogh.

He's doing it now as we sit at the kitchen table stirring our drinks.

"You know, Van Gogh painted for ten years and only sold one painting." He says

"Yeah Dad, I'm not exactly Van Gogh."

He goes on to say, "A Confederacy of Dunces was published eleven years after John Kennedy Toole's suicide."

"Dad, Walker Percy died in 1990."

"Why do you have to be so morbid all the time?" he says as he stirs his tea with a pencil. "Is it because I use to let you kids poke dead things with sticks?"

"Dad, it was Missouri. Everybody poked dead things with sticks."

He laughs again uncomfortably, probably flashing back to all the times he and the other parents would see a parade of children looking like a scene out of *Lord of the Flies*, each with a wooden spear.

"Where you kids going?" They would yell.

And we'd scream, "Nathan found a dead raccoon by the tracks. We're gonna go poke it."

I think My father hates my obsession with death.

I try to remind him I've always been a strange kid.

"Oh you mean that time when you were seven and we found you in the coat closet covered in ketchup and bacon bits?

You said you were pretending to be eaten by ticks." He says, "We thought it was an isolated incident you know, a kid just being a kid."

My next fake-death took place in a neighbor's aboveground pool. I used a red-and-white bendy-straw for a breathing apparatus. My blonde hair panned across the chlorine waters while my tank top rode up my belly, stopping at my armpits. After that, there was the time I rigged a coat hanger to make it look like I had hung myself on a door, and my personal favorite, an intricate charcoal drawing on my stomach to represent a tire track, my body lifeless on the asphalt, all before the age of ten.

My father walks over to the microwave and begins to zap his tea. I pull the Vonnegut book out of my back pocket and place it on the table. He turns around eyeing it, happy at the possibility of a change in subject.

"Ahh excellent choice, nothing like revisiting a classic." He says

I feel ashamed of the Joe Hill novel on my nightstand back home.

"Listen Dad I've thought a lot about this. It's what I want."

He turns back to the microwave and impatiently waits for the tea to stop spinning on the plastic tray. He knows what's coming; we've had this conversation before. There was the time I went to Film and Esthiology School, was a touring musician, jewelry maker, apprenticed to be a piercer, wanted to be a painter, and then became a business owner (all while trying to pen the next Great American Novel).

"I thought you wanted to be a writer?"

"I do, I did, I love writing, but Dad this whole struggling artist thing it's..."

"It's romantic isn't it?" He says interrupting me.

"Dad listen, I've made my decision and I hope you can support me. I'm tired of being poor."

He shakes his head and picks up the Vonnegut book and runs his fingers over the red tape holding the spine together. He pages through it and sets it on the marble table and sighs.

2

The Destination Forest

It took two days to bury him. He was my best and only friend. I couldn't tell any of the kids at school, and I dared not tell my parents. It was an accident, I swear. We were just playing, Jake and me. My older brother, Jimmy, was at hockey practice; Mom and Dad were still at work. The blood was everywhere. It splattered on my face and turned the grass a deep brown. I ran to the bathroom, tore off my clothes, and jumped into the shower. I scrubbed and scrubbed and scrubbed, but the blood stayed beneath my fingernails. I found Jimmy's old hockey bag, the one with the frayed green handle. I was greeted by a horrifying smell, like that fancy cheese Mom serves at dinner parties. My nose wrinkled with disgust, and I had to put my elbow over my face. I threw my bloodstained clothes into the bag and made my way back to the place where I had killed Jake.

I rolled him over with my foot, his pink tongue-hanging limp out of his mouth like a small piece of wet taffy. He barely fit in the bag. I lifted it with a heave and set it back down with a ho. I grabbed the garden hose and watched the brown and red discoloration seep into the dirt. I lapped at the water running from the hose as it trickled to a stop.

I was sweating before I left the driveway. Large dark circles began to form under my arms. My blue and red striped shirt crawled up my large belly. My black-rimmed glasses slid down my pig nose.

Pig Nose is what all the kids call me at school, sometimes on special occasions Fatty Ferguson, Fat Fuck Faggot, or Queer. Mostly it's just Pig Nose; they've been calling me that for years.

Mom used to say I'd thin out over time, though not so much now that I'm twelve going on thirteen. I've been fat since I can remember (or "husky," in Dad's words).

Jimmy's sixteen and swears I'm adopted. He's tall and slender, his blonde hair is cut so a chunk can cover his left eye. He'll swing that lock, and, man, the girls go crazy. Jimmy's had more girlfriends than I can count on both my hands!

Mom is blonde like Jimmy and hates when his friends call her a *MILF* (he told me it means "Mom I'd Like to Fuck"). Dad doesn't have hair, but I'm sure he'd be considered a *DILF*. I can hear him every other morning shaving his head with the clippers before work. He's tan with broad shoulders, and sometimes when he drinks, he likes to pull out old photos of himself to show his two sons "what a stud" he was in college. When this happens, my Mom likes to kiss his shiny head and remind him he still is.

Jimmy says maybe kids would be nicer to me if "I didn't dress like such a dweeb." He even convinced me not to wear my really cool eyeglass strap. It's camouflaged, with one retractable brown bead.

I knew exactly where I was going. We (Jake and I) used to go there all the time. We'd build forts under the trees, read comic books and drink sodas, and I'd tell him everything. Nobody but him and me knew about this place. I guess now it's just me.

I shifted the weight of the bag back and forth between my arms. God he was heavy, but not heavier than me.

The Destination Forest (that's what we called it) was seven and a half blocks away. I took side streets not to draw attention to the fat kid and his bag, but there was no avoiding the corner store. I suppose I could go around, but that would take more time. If I wasn't home for dinner, Mom would kill me, Dad would worry, and Jimmy would get suspicious.

I should have run, but Jake was too heavy. He started to leave large indentations on both my shoulders. I could feel the salty liquid piling up in my neck and stomach rolls.

"Keep your head down, you fat son-of-a-bitch," I said to myself under my breath.

They were always up there. When I was with Jake, they usually left me alone.

I set the bag down ten feet away. I took off my glasses and began to rub them with the bottoms of my sweat-soaked shirt. I felt like a soldier preparing for battle in a war I was sure to lose. I took one deep breath and puffed out my chest.

Shitty-shithead Chris McGee was the first to spot me. He was leaning against the side of the store, flinging his curly brown shag while flipping his skateboard with his left foot. God he was cool. I couldn't deny that. He was with his usual four friends. Jake and I called them "The McGee Minions," always following his lead, doing what he said. Total assholes.

"Maybe they won't see me?" I said to Jake's corpse.

I stood out like a Sasquatch. My pace slowed and I continued to look at my feet.

"Hey, pig nose! Come back for more? "

Chris dropped his bag of Red Hot Flaming Cheetos. They spilt onto the sidewalk reminding me of Jake's blood on the green grass. He skateboarded over with his four friends closely behind. They made a circle around me. I was a piece of meat dropped into shark-infested waters awaiting the feeding frenzy.

"What's in the bag, pig nose?" Chris said.

I tried to keep walking but it was no use; minion number three pushed, and I fell to the ground, my tooth colliding with my lip. Jake fell, too.

"Come on, you fat fuck. Tell him what's in the bag."

Minion two kicked me in my stomach. I tried to block him as my belly jiggled in my hand. You'd think it wouldn't hurt as much, my fat rolls protecting my guts. But it did. The ripple of my blubber made me want to puke.

When these things happen -- getting punched, kicked or shoved -- I find myself going into a trance or mantra (that's what my mom says they call it in yoga class). It starts with six words, and then rapidly turns into two. "Don't let them see you cry. Don't cry. Don't cry. Don't cry."

Minion number one joined in with a few kicks.

"I bet it's a dead body," He said to Chris with a grin.

"It's pig nose, he's so fucking weird. Aren't cha, fatty?"

Oh my god! How did he know? My face turned red. He rolled me over with his foot just like I had done to Jake an hour earlier. I was a bloated whale washed ashore with my hands over my head.

I watched Chris walk over to the bag and squat. His jean shorts rode up his leg to show a hairy thigh. (He already had leg hair!) He lifted the bag for a second to see what it weighed, then dropped it dangerously close to my head.

"It's heavy," he said to his shithead friends.

He began to finger the black painted zipper. I stood up as fast as a beaten-down fat kid could. Then I reached over Jake and pushed. With every muscle in my body, I shoved shitty-shithead Chris McGee. He fell on his back, and I thought I heard the concrete break.

Earlier that day in school he'd beaten me good. I was in the bathroom taking a pee when he came up from behind. He was a gladiator whipping a black backpack at my head, and I, the innocent man shoved into the arena. My glasses flew into the urinal (but thankfully didn't break). I was mid-stream and peed on my pants, new shoes, socks and my hand. He kicked me four times as I covered my head. I stayed in the stall with my feet on the toilet seat for all of second period blowing on the urine stains and praying they'd dry before gym.

The funny thing is Chris used to be my best friend, before I met Jake. He lived two doors down. This was before junior high, skateboards, minions, and girls. We had sleepovers and spent hours on our walkie-talkies (if you stood in a certain spot in the backyard, they really worked). He was the guest of honor at my birthday parties and I at his. He really was coolest kid I knew.

I'm not sure why we stopped being friends; I guess we just did. Mom says it's because he's a "little asshole" just like his "good-for-nothing father," who doesn't live down the street.

Chris tried to stand up, and what I did next was this: I grabbed that hairy leg of his and swung. Round and around like the ice skaters do with their female partners. I was a warrior, and he was my axe. For the first time in my life, I fought back.

I dropped him on the pavement and scooped Jake into my arms, and ran as fast as I could until I reached our special place, the biggest tree in the woods, the one that I carved *Jake + Josh 4eva* into the bark.

I looked around for an open spot to bury the broken bag filled with my bloody clothes and Jake. I found a nice plot of land, a perfect place to dig a grave, and then it dawned on me. Shit. A shovel.

I couldn't just leave him, or bring him all the way back home.

So I dug with the same hands that had killed Jake. I dug till my fingers bled. I dug until the dirt covered every inch of my arms, neck, and chest. I dug until it was thick in my nails and nose, and then I dug some more.

It was a shallow grave no deeper than my forearm. I pushed Jake inside and covered him with dirt. It looked like the giant mud pies I used to make with Chris when we were six.

I could barely see five feet in front of me. I checked my trusty compass and said one last thing to Jake: "I promise you, Jake, I'll be back tomorrow, and I swear to god I'll bring a shovel."

I ran as fast as a covered-in-mud-and-blood fat kid could. No one was at the corner store, and only two jerks honked their horns.

His and hers Volvos were in the driveway. I tried to slink through the front door and tiptoe up the stairs.

"Hey, big guy, where you been?" My dad scratched the top of my prickly crew cut. Dirt trickled to the floor. He scrunched up his nose and pulled back his head until a double chin appeared.

"What the hell? Josh, why are you covered in dirt?"

I pushed away his hand and jogged up the stairs, his voice trailing behind.

"Josh, answer me. Were you out with Jake?" Hearing someone say Jake's name for the first time today made my heart hurt. I slammed the bathroom door. The crash made me jump.

My father yelled one last thing. He said, "Josh where's Jake?"

I stripped off my clothes again, this time covered in dirt. The water beat on my back and stung my cut-up hands and head. There was no distinction between the water and my tears. I cry a lot in private. I cried for Chris, and I cried for myself, and I wept with guilt for Jake.

We were playing catch in the backyard, like we always did, Jake and me, laughing, and chatting, and eating ice cream. Then just like Chris, Jake suddenly turned on me. He had this crazed look in his eye. Then he bit my hand. I picked up the closest rock I could find, and I hit him in the head. The blood began to pour out of his nose, and I hit him again and again and again, until all I could see was nothingness.

He just lay there, lifeless, his head turning to mush. I kept swinging that rock as hard as any beaten-down fat kid could.

I know when I get out of the shower I will have to answer to my parents. I have a few alibis and lies that will probably work, but all I can think about is poor Jake alone, half-buried in the woods. He was my best and only friend.

3

The Day My Brother Borrowed My Car

You don't notice it at first. You have to squint or put your nose dangerously close to see them. It's as though someone dipped a fine brush into brown paint and flicked it on the steering wheel of your car; a microscopic Jackson Pollack piece staring back at you as you sit at a red light.

"Is it blood? " I ask my parents. They stare down at their feet and shift uncomfortably. I've seen these splatters before on two different cars and several bathroom walls.

My father and I go down to his office and I set the recorder between us. He shifts uncomfortably. The red light blinks. He begins by saying, " Your brother is doing a lot better."

His body tightens. His words are defensive. I remind him the spots on the steering wheel of my car are recent, within the last two weeks.

My only brother is two years younger than me. At thirty-two years old he has become a stocky, well built man. He is handsome with brown eyes that match his short kept hair. He prefers nonfiction history to fiction. I've seen him pick up and play with ease almost every musical instrument. As a child I remember struggling through each piano lesson, studying the sheet music until my head hurt, practicing for hours. I resented him for never needing to. He would stroll in after my lesson calm and cool and play the same song with elegance and ease, all by just listening to it once. He is a man of many talents. He is also a drug addict.

I tap my pencil on the yellow legal pad. My family prefers not to talk about my brother's disease.

"It *is* a disease." my mother likes to remind me.

This was back when I fought for the truth, wait to catch him in a lie, point with an accusatory finger when his eyes and head would grow heavy as sweat covered his face during Christmas dinner, watch him drool on himself next to me on a plane, after spending twenty five minutes in a LAX airport bathroom waiting for a connecting flight for a week long family vacation.

My mom would say, "It's his allergy medicine" or "food poisoning." If it is the latter, my brother has had food poisoning more than humanly possible. I ask my father to check his own car for bloodstains on the steering wheel. We do it together as a family, the three of us, my mother, father and I. The interior in the first car is too dark. I swear I see something, my mother swears she doesn't and my father decides to be distracted by a leaf blower on a shelf.

My mother and I sit at a restaurant as she explains to me what the splatters on our car's steering columns are.

"It's not blood," She says, she swabbed it once out of curiosity. (The benefits of having worked in a lab for so many years.) She takes the spoon off the table and pretends to hold a lighter under it. "It's the heroin splattering while he cooks it. " she says

She goes on to say that he's doing better. Instead of finding bags of dirty syringes, now she only finds a few. These bantam Pollack paintings that once filled her bathroom walls now only make occasional appearances in our cars.

Her eyes gaze through the cracks of the patio table we sit at. She sets the spoon down and wipes her aging face with a white paper napkin. She pushes her food around and tries to change the subject,

"Are you excited for your move?"

Her face looks old. I see myself, a mixture of my fate, my fears, and failings.

She is my future. She is me.

It's been two weeks and I have yet to clean the heroin off the steering wheel of my car. Maybe I never will. For years I tried to uncover the truth about my brothers addiction and pull my parents from the depths of denial. It is at this moment I realize we are in a much darker place. We have now succumbed to acceptance.

4

The First Time I Partied

The blood feels warm dripping out my nose. The mixture of iron and salt fills the divots of my chapped lips. My right eye springs open.

The left eye is swollen shut. I try to pull my arms down to assess the damages done to my face but can't. They are tied over my head. I am 13 years old.

The man responsible is kneeling next to the bed. One of his hands grips my right calf; the other descends into a dim abyss between his legs. The rising sun breaks through the cracks of the off-white plastic curtains, illuminating the stains on the beige carpet. His movements are repetitive. His back heaves the same way my family dog's does after consuming too much grass. It is an action I've never seen a man do before. A violent shiver possesses his body and he collapses. I wait until he stops moving. His face is buried in a thick arm.

It *is* like in the movies. If you wiggle and pull, no matter how bad it hurts, you will get loose. I see my friend Stacy that morning on the living room floor. I shake her with urgency. She awakes with a twitch.

Stacy is 16. (She draws navy-blue circles around her eyes every morning.) Traces of her pink lip-gloss can be found on Mountain Dew cans and Marlboro Light 100's. We arrive at her house. I rinse the blood off my face. I poke holes the size of my thumbs into the cuffs of one of her long-sleeved shirts to cover the red rings around my wrists. She hands me a tube of dark lipstick and I use it to fill my split lip. She sits me on the toilet and begins to rub, pat, and powder the yellow, blue and green, discolorations around my eye.

*   *   *

One year later I am in eighth grade. I dye my hair green and get my first tattoo. My grades start to slip and I'm no longer allowed to be the captain of the softball team. I am asked to step down as president of the student counsel and expelled two weeks later. I spend my 15th birthday in a lock-up treatment facility for drug addicts. My father is sent to an adult center a few weeks later for alcoholism. He stops referring to me as *his* daughter. I am a disappointment, a crusher of dreams.

*   *   *

I awake in a hospital bed, my parents hovering over me. Both their arms are crossed; mine are strapped to the bed. It is my third failed suicide attempt. I am 17 years old. They can't take it anymore, the drugs, the drinking, the running away, missing for days, and the suicide attempts. I am a delinquent and must be sent away. So I am.

*   *   *

It is a year later. I am 18. I am sober. I see therapists that make me take little pink pills so I won't hurt myself. I am better.

My mother is the first person I tell my secret to. I phone her unexpectedly. I let the phone cord coil around my finger as I tell her what happened. I think she is crying, but I can't tell.

*   *   *

I am 21 when I decide to tell my father. I am drunk off of two bottles of wine. He is filled with pasta and soda water. I tell him in a restaurant as I blow smoke in his face. I smirk with delight watching his body contort with my choice of words. I shake my head to provoke shame and imply, he should have seen the signs. I tell him to be cruel, to get back at him, and for once to feel like I, yes I, have the upper hand.

* * *

People I know speak freely about losing their virginity. It's a common topic tossed around at parties. I shake ever so slightly when the person-to-person story gets closer to me. I stare at my feet trying to time my bathroom breaks accordingly. Sometimes my turn is inevitable.

* * *

I cannot forget my mother telling me to eat my supper, as I counted quarters under the table, hoping to buy a burger later. The sound of Stacy's car horn in our driveway. The way the air felt between my fingers as we cruised up and down the midway. The queasiness I felt when the two older men pulled up to the car and said, "You girls wanna go to a party?"

The dread I felt when Stacy said, " We'll stay for one drink then leave. Okay?"

The moment I said, "Okay."

The way my body shivered when we got to the apartment and realized it was a party of four.

How my voice trembled when the strange man brought out two drinks, one for each girl, and I looked at Stacy and said, "One drink, right?"

How she nodded in agreement, and the evening disappeared.

* * *

What I choose to remember of that day is this: The sun on my freckled shoulders. The glow of the green algae covering the lake as the smell of dead fish stung my nose. My blonde hair pulled into a tight ponytail. One freshly oiled baseball glove with *R. Puskas* written in permanent marker on the outside thumb. My hand pulling the ball from my left, releasing, and watching it ascend into the sky, and my father standing in silence, across from me, waiting, punching his glove and smiling.

5

Tiny Braids

Baby arm is what we called it. It was the size of a novelty baseball bat one could win at a fair. The skin connecting it to his shoulder was the same circumference as his wrist. The red scars that started at his shoulder and ended at his elbow ran across each other like yarn in a knitted sweater.

He would plop down on a chair and kick one leg over the other, grab the baby arm with his left hand and swing it across his lap. His functioning hand had dirt under the nails and calluses covering the palm, it was a grown man's hand, holding onto a child's arm. His t-shirt sleeve wrapped around his left bicep as if it were going to rip at any moment, while the right one hung down like a white flag trying to induce a truce.

His first name was Nathan, but everyone called him Posso. His teeth were mustard yellow. His sandy blonde hair looked three shades darker from the lack of washing.

"Oh Yuck, this smells like Posso" could be heard when describing an unfavorable odor.

Some people were scared of him; others called him a-piece-of-shit, loser, thief, drunk, mooch, asshole, or a prick. I would see him at parties and turn up my nose and avoid eye contact. If I saw him walk in the front door of a public place, I would slyly slip out the back.

The first time we spoke I was 23, working at a run down coffee shop, and he was 21; yet to have a job.

"You gotta an extra cigarette?" he said.

The fear in my eyes was apparent. I set my book down, and pushed the cigarette pack his way. Posso grabbed it with his good hand, using his mouth to open it. His yellow teeth bit down on one of the cigarettes and yanked. He smirked as the flame lit the tip and I couldn't help but cringe.

"Everything was beautiful, and nothing hurt." He said.

The smoke curled around his nose as it pushed out his mouth.

"What did you just say?"

"It's my favorite line from that book you're reading."

He pulled a sharpie out of his pocket and proceeded to write something on the wooden picnic table.

"You've read Vonnegut?" I said

My voice heightened with disbelief and judgment. He was writing with such intensity that I could see the sharpie sinking into the rotting wood.

"Yeah, of course I have. He's not my all time favorite, but he's pretty alright. I like that guy…um..uh Phillip K. Dick, and what's his name, god damnit, shit.. Kafka, that guy, his shit is great."

Posso finished his cigarette and flicked it into the street. He traced the word on the table one last time before putting the cap on the marker with his lips. My head cocked to try and read the upside down writing.

"Licknuts." He said pulling up his shirt to show me the same word tattooed across his stomach.

Posso started to come into the coffee shop a lot after that. He would sit with me throughout my entire shift, talking about books he'd read, girls he had crushes on, or trips he wanted to take. If I'd work late he'd always come in at close and haul out the trash, so I wouldn't have to go into the alley alone.

I learned Posso didn't really have a family; he'd been homeless since he was thirteen. I would take him to my parent's house for the holidays; Easter, Thanksgiving, and the Fourth of July, but never on Christmas, he chose to spend that one alone with a bottle of whiskey.

One Thanksgiving I finally mustered up enough courage to ask him what happened to his arm; he took off his shirt and let me touch his scars.

He was fifteen, drunk and high, tagging a parked train with a friend.

"I remember the light of the passing train. The ground and metal rails under my spine, my friend screaming, and then the right side of my body gone."

He spent the next year in a hospital bed, in his words, "on a shit ton of morphine" as the doctors tried to reattach his arm.

The last time I saw Posso was two years ago. I no longer worked at the coffee shop, but now owned a salon down the street. He came by looking hungry, as if he hadn't slept in days. His long greasy hair clung to his sunken cheeks, and a few of his yellow teeth had fallen out. I could smell the alcohol on his breath and see the track marks on his arms. He asked me if I could wash his hair like I use to, and put it into braids.

The waiting room was filled with suburban woman impatient for their foils and cuts. I looked at Posso that day with the same disgust as the first time we met and turned him away.

Posso took his own life this year. He was thirty-one years old. He shot himself in a YMCA, in front of a locker possessing everything he owned.

Sometimes I lay awake at night and pretend I would've said yes. "Yes, of course Posso, please, come in. Sit down."

I'd shampoo his hair twice to make sure it was extra clean. I'd bring him back to the chair and put in two French braids, "make em really tight" he'd say "so they last a couple of weeks".

He would tell me all about the books he was reading, girls he had crushes on, and all the cities he wanted to see. I would tie the braids up with two little black rubber bands, and lightly tug on them before he would leave.

Maybe he would bum one more cigarette or apologize for losing the last book I lent him, or maybe he would just peddle away, as I stood outside like a worried mother, and he would turn back at me smiling, his baby arm swaying in the wind, waving, as if to gesture, go on, go on, I got this, I promise I'm gonna be okay.

6

The Time I Went to Writing School and My Teacher Hated Me

The six playing cards stick together in her hand. She peels them off one-by-one holding them over her mouth so he can't see the ends of her lips curl upward in satisfaction. Her smile fades as she sees a six, a three, a four, a king, a queen, and a seven fanned over her left palm.

They sit at a booth in the kitchen. A picture of a favorite nephew and an old black-and-white photo of his mother share a magnet in the shape of an anchor on the buzzing refrigerator door. She lightly places the king and queen facedown in front of him. She can't help but think he'll get the subtleties behind the couple she chose to offer.

When she's had too much scotch, the small triangle patterns on the Formica table, swirl into one another, building stronger shapes with heavier lines. When this happens she likes to slide her thumb over the chrome siding until the ridges leave bright red indents that she can caress under the table.

His wedding ring is sitting on the mantle next to a bottle of cologne, and a framed photo of his dead brother. She remembers the day he took off the ring and stopped smelling of musk. She's only met his estranged wife once. Was she a blonde or a brunette? Sometimes when he's drunk he'll tell her stories about how his wife is an executive chef at a popular restaurant, the awards she won, and the sacrifices she's made for her career. After these drunken rants, his brown eyes turn black, his elongated sentences turn into two word responses, and his proud stiff back goes slack.

He uses hand gestures to emphasize each syllable. A finger taps on the table to punctuate anger. Two fingers on each hand fan back-and-forth like arms in a pinball machine when a series of emotions can't be relayed with words.

They've been sitting at this table playing cribbage every other night for six months. It's a casual thing, a partnership without the paperwork.

She lays the first card down.

"Six?"

He raises a dark brow over one eye, pulls a card, and drops it steadily on the table. She glares at his six of hearts, hoping it will catch on fire.

"Twelve for two." He smiles. She thinks he has perfect teeth.

"Goddamnit."

He smirks at her reaction. She can tell he wants to say something. She avoids eye contact and lays down her four.

"Sixteen?"

Her voice heightens as she questions her math skills. He nods in agreement and sets down a seven. Sometimes when it's her turn to use the bathroom she makes him stand in the hallway of his recently signed two-year rental. She doesn't want him to hear her in such a vulnerable state. She likes to look for faces in the gold patterns on the shower tiles hiding behind the clear curtain.

They both have two stacks of cards in front of them. She nods and rubs the last two in her hand.

"Twenty-six?" This time she poses it as a question in hopes of him not trumping her failed hand.

"That's a go."

She sighs and sets down her last card, placing the peg one move up. He laughs at how dramatically the air escapes her mouth. His hands are confident as he slaps, not lays, an eight of hearts abruptly on the table.

"That's fifteen for two, and one for last card."

"I know what it is."

"Are you mad?" He's trying to be funny.

"No. Just count already."

She looks at her hand and sucks in the sides of her cheeks until her teeth have hold of the pink flesh, chewing and gnawing as if it's a filet mignon she can't swallow. He's tapping on the table again with his pointer fingers, this time with fervor.

It started a week ago, the daydreaming of the two of them frolicking through the pastures of life hand-in-hand. She thinks of it now as he counts out loud.

"Fifteen two, fifteen four, fifteen six, trips for six more…"

She interrupts him, rudely, thoughtlessly, "It's twenty-one. You have twenty-one."

She imagines them dating in public. Not like they do now in a hidden one-bedroom apartment between the hours of midnight and noon. No she imagines movie-dates and dinners, breakfasts, lunches, and brunches with well received intermingled friends.

She thinks of these things and smiles, despite the shitty cards cuffed in her hand. She looks up. He's smiling too. He's in a black t-shirt and jeans, his grandfather's old silver watch heavy on his wrist. Her shoulders are hunched as she absently twists a brown strand of hair around her pointer finger.

She imagines their first potential apartment, a staggering two bedroom in the heart of uptown. Maybe in a duplex, or quiet fourplex where other like-minded couples live, fornicate, and invite them over for extravagant dinner parties and screenings of art house films you can only find on raremovies.com. They would hold h...

fabled move googling Feng Shui, the art ...

The bedroom would be a chocolat...

ment and sensual energy). The kitchen ye...

office an orange (to represent warmth a...

entangled in sheets and legs and sex and...

The day of the fanciful move wou...

neatly stacked in their proper rooms. The...

an element of accommodation.

"Whatever you think."

"No I think that looks great right there." These statements would be said between kisses, caresses, butt-pats, and hair-pulls.

Their first fight would ensue over a placement of art. He would set down the clothes, dishes, or box of miscellaneous things and storm out of the room. Why? Because this is the way first fights unfold, pointless, dramatic, endearing and inevitable. They would make-up in the futuristic bed lined with sheets they picked out together. A set of pale blue 600 Egyptian-thread count, an expensive splurge in celebration of their new union.

She looks up at him in his real-life kitchen and tries to reintegrate herself in the present moment. He's glowing with pride at his remarkable lead on the cribbage board while waiting for her to count. She doesn't. Instead she stares out the window across the snow-covered ground. When she thinks too hard about their predicament she can't help but imagine kicking out the glass pane and sliding down the two blue cables swinging between the complexes. The community grill for the apartment building is a white-capped piece of coal.

She closes her eyes and goes back to their fictional lives, no, their future lives. She's in their apartment again waiting for him to come home from work, cooking the only thing she knows how to make, chili. The cans of beans, tomatoes, and peppers are emptied and tossed into the grocery

ing this isn't cooking. She has browned the beef for

outsides now crunchy and burnt.

es when she tries to cook or play the role of a domesticated

She's not and he can't help but hate that about her too. He never

that, not directly, but she can see it in his eyes when she attempts to

clean the bathroom, or when she says, "I made dinner." Which in translation means a family-sized pouch of pre-made pasta from the freezer section dumped into a pot, which she still manages to overcook, in the end serving mushy white noodles floating in a watery sauce on his plate.

She doesn't need him to say the words as his fork pushes around the food for ten minutes before getting up for a whiskey and retreating to the living room to watch basketball. He'd never had an interest in sports. Now he buys season tickets with his friends. They liked to get dinner afterwards at the strip clubs conveniently placed next to the arenas.

They are technically not allowed to smoke in his apartment. The one they are presently playing cards in. Yet every time he gets enough whiskey in his system the window comes up, propped by an ivory-handled knife, and they puff away blowing smoke towards the cold air.

She's doing it now, smoking a lease-breaking cigarette as he sits smiling, patiently waiting for her to come back to the game, come back to him. She pulls a drag and flashes forward one last time.

It's the chili night again. She's leaning out their shared made-up kitchen window smoking in defiance to their imaginary lease of their fictional apartment. He was supposed to be home two hours ago. She places a hand on the ten pounds she's gained sense they've been living together, one year, six months and two days.

They don't have sex much anymore, too tired, too late, somebody's got to get up early, the list as long as her cigarette ash growing towards her finger. Instead of staring out a kitchen window at three in the morning over a game of cards, she now stares out of a bedroom window next to a snoring man.

The key jiggles in the lock and she knows he's been drinking, his feet heavy on each stair. He looks at her with tired bloodshot eyes.

"Chili again huh? Shocking. I already ate." He stumbles to the icebox and drops three ice cubes into a low-ball before swaying into the living room.

She opens her eyes and finds herself back at the Formica tabletop covered in cards and a cribbage board, whiskey glasses and a coffee mug filled with cigarette butts.

"Are you gonna count your hand or what? Come on sweetie, we ain't got all night." He winks at her.

She thinks about his love of country music and sad movies. How he gets worked up over political situations, his drunken outbursts of family secrets and past relationships, and his idiotic theory on why he doesn't own a computer. She thinks of these things and wants nothing more than to lean over the table and kiss each line forming around his eyes, wrap her hand around his tapping finger, cup his drooping jowl, and caress his thick black hair.

She makes eye contact for the first time in this round of cribbage. He doesn't flinch but instead meets her gaze with confidence and possibly concern. She sets her four cards down, exactly one inch apart, one six of clubs, one three of hearts, one four of spades, and one seven of diamonds and says, "I got nothing."

"Nothing?"

"Zero."

He shakes his head in apathy. She remembers in the beginning she would confuse it with empathy. He hands over the cards and cracks a joke about how he loves when she gets "card-mad."

As she shuffles, a few cards slip out of the pile and land on the floor, he bends down to grab them. His head pops up as he reaches for her fist full of cards. She taps her finger on the table the same way she's seen him do so many times. She sighs on accident and turns back to the window.

A light turns on in the apartment across the yard. A man walks from his bedroom to the kitchen. He pours a glass of water and sits at a table, He's large and balding, shirtless in loose fitting boxers. She spreads her hand against the glass panel, leaving four streaks like racing tracks down the frosted pane. She wants him to notice her. He doesn't, not once; instead he finishes his water, stands, scratches his ass and walks back to bed.

7

The Rapper

You wake up on the floor because it wasn't your turn to get a bed. You run to the bathroom before the other four people in the room begin to stir. You shit and piss; masturbate in the shower. This will be your only moment of solace.

Soon someone begins to pound on the locked bathroom door. A muffled conversation can be heard in the other room, something about check-out time, sound check, and how long it'll take to get to the next city?

You stopped wearing underwear, you haven't had a chance to do laundry in weeks. You pull up the stiff smelling jeans, one of two pairs you packed.

No sooner does the button lock make a subtle pop are you pushed out of the way to make room for another band member to violate the bathroom in the same way.

You stand outside the hotel trying to remember how you ended up there last night. You can't. You reach into your pocket to see if you have money for a coffee.

You don't.

You pile in the van. The tour manager yells, "Come on guys, we gotta go! Fuck where's Jake? Has anyone seen him since last night?"

Jake is a replaceable name on any given night. At least one band member disappears. A girl, some drugs, an opportunity to sleep in a bed, while wives and girlfriends sleep soundly at home.

You average four to five hours of sleep a night.

Your throat and head hurts.

Your stomach growls in pain from the masses of shitty food and beer you've consumed and will continue to consume for the rest of the tour. You learn to love ramen, crunching up the bag and sprinkling the MSG onto the dry noodles, and eating it like a bag of chips.

The van smells like rotten food, body odor, stinky feet, stale beer, weed, and Doritos.

You stopped being able to smell it three weeks in. It's only when a random photographer, journalist, or the occasional groupie point it out does it once again sting your nose.

Sometimes you don't get a hotel room or an option to sleep anywhere other then in the six-passenger van that smells like shit.

No time for stopping. The booking agent cut the next show too close.

You sweat and bleed, scream and get drunk, only to get back in the van and drive ten hours to the next venue in some shit town.

Your girlfriend calls and you send her directly to voicemail. You can't tell her how bad you want to come home in front of the other guys, you don't want to lie about the things you've seen or done, and you won't because your band members will always remind you "what goes on the road stays on the road". Sometimes venues are desolate, ten people stand, staring blankly, as the sound-man rolls his eyes.

Others are packed, filled with adoring fans, screaming your name, begging for autographs, waiting outside for hours to catch a glimpse of their idol, to sleep with their crush, to tell you,

"You changed their lives" and they "relate to your lyrics and heart-break". They want to tell you their story, give you *their* CD. They swarm like hornets, buzzing in your ear.

If you move too fast they'll sting all at once. If you stay too still you will never escape.

You hate your band-mates.

You hate your fans.

Your arm sticks to the un-showered guy next to you who smells like pennies and whiskey. You tilt your head left then right to try and get comfortable. You ask yourself why? Why are you here? You remind yourself that very few make it in the music industry. You tell yourself to never stop treading water because if you do hundreds will be waiting below. Wanting nothing more than to grab your leg like frenzied sharks shaking, their desperate teeth yanking at your limp body, pulling you down to the depths of normalcy never to be heard from again.

You think about that normalcy with envy. You lust for it, until you finally receive it, a week after your homecoming. When the laundry has been clean. The bills have piled up. The adoring fans have disappeared. The sex with your girlfriend has been exhausted. The conversations about, "how was tour?" become mundane and repetitive. You begin to fight with your girlfriend because she doesn't understand why you have to leave "again" and why you find yourself agreeing to another six-month tour around the Midwest. It's a catch 22, and you laugh at the fact your girlfriend asked you to read that book two months before you left, and you lied and said you did, and loved it.

8

The Itch

David has an itch. It's a tingling that starts in his bones and spills into his veins. It crawls in his skin all afternoon.

He scratches and rubs, but it never subsides. It's hard for him to concentrate at school. His Sixteen year old body shakes during a second period math quiz, and he decides to sit alone at lunch.

David sweats profusely under his catcher gear. That afternoon after classes. He can't focus. He squats at the tip of the diamond blinking, trying to concentrate on the teammate across from him whipping a baseball at his crotch. His coach yells "David, get your head in the game!"

He fumbles during two crucial moments; one leaves him running down the foul ball line like a bumbling idiot as two runners round home for the winning scores. (It's a varsity vs junior varsity, and his mistakes make him the butt of his fellow varsity mates.)

His teammates blame him. David blames the itch.

He packs his gear into the brown canvas bag and shoves it into the locked cage. He kicks off his cleats and places them under the bench in the locker room. No one says a word as he strips off his clothes and hangs his head.

David rarely took showers after games or practices. There's something machismo about the scent of victory, or the smell of defeat.

Yet now, as the water pelted his back, he pictured Lila's perfect (turned sixteen today) breasts in a shower as well, dripping with water, her lips damp and quivering.

Before today his feelings for his neighbor Lila had been separate elements, neatly compartmentalized.

Sympathy was the first. Or was it pity?

Happiness transpired, followed by gratitude. As David grew older and his body rapidly produced testosterone, adoration and euphoria made a well-woven monolithic ball in his gut.

Today was the day. The itch would stop. He towels himself off, throws a t-shirt and jeans on and leaves his dingy uniform on the red bench.

He goes unnoticed as he enters her house, running straight to Lila's bedroom.

David takes Lila's hand and leads her down the stairs to the fenced-in back yard. They sit cross-legged in the soft grass, knees touching at the caps.

He places his hand on her olive shoulder and gently pinches the bone. He's never touched her like that. He can't believe he's doing it now, but he can't stop.

Today was the day; there was no going back. David pushes Lila's hair out of her face. The silky brown locks slip through his fingers. He rests his callused hand on her scarred cheek. He searches her eyes and reminds himself she's his best friend. David leans in until his lips touch hers.

The electric shock that hit him the first time they met, came shooting back. Bolt after bolt. For the first time in her presence, he shook. His entire body ruptured with tremors.

In that instant David finds himself embracing a statue. She doesn't respond to the kiss. Her face is tense.

A tear begins to roll down her cheek and onto his lips. He savors the salty flavor on his tongue. The tear slips down his throat. The watery seed of guilt drops into the pit of his stomach. He can feel it spread to his limbs. His fingers. His toes. The infected tear pumps upward to his brain. Where it rests. He opens his eyes, drops his hands and looks for her gaze. Lila's eyes are sunk into the grass. Her irises planted in the dirt.

Just like that, the orb of emotions begins to dissipate and form separate unions.

Embarrassment (or was it shame?) sinks its claws deep into David's thighs and pulls with all its might. He stumbles onto his arms. He glides backwards on the grass. Embarrassment yanks his body into a standing position and shoves.

He takes one last look at Lila and runs, past the yard, over the driveway, and a long way from home. He runs until his heart becomes a tight knot. His lungs flash warning signs of failure, and his tears no longer recognizable amidst the drops of sweat.

That's when David's feet stop. His hands brace his knees. A python of anger swallows up his mousy feeling of embarrassment. He succumbs to it, and lets the anger carry him home.

9

The Accused

PART I

I can smell him on the pillow before I open my eyes. I vomit on the side of the bed. The first thing I see is the liquid seep into the cracks of the wooden floor. I grab the vacant pillow and use it to soak up the vile. I will burn it, I decide.

The phone vibrates next to my head. Four missed calls blink on the screen before it goes black. I only leave my bed for two reasons, to use the bathroom, and to shower. The sound of the water running behind me is soothing, repetitive, and clean. The steam lightly coats the mirror as my arms straddle the sink.

The woman staring back is a stranger. She smells of booze and her nose is crusted with blood. Two black and blue handprints circle her neck.I lay my hands over the women in the mirror's bruises to see if they'll match up. The act reminds me of jigsaw puzzles, my favorite childhood pastime.

She is saying something in the mirror, whispering, pointing.

She says, "You are strong and brave. You are a survivor and you would never let this happen to you."

I take off my shirt. The same bruised handprints appear on my arms. I hold my hair in my hand, and let myself vomit.

I can hear the phone ringing in the other room.

The guilt consumes my body. I shake.

I crawl into the bathtub. The water beats against my back. I trace the dirt ring around the tub with my finger. I scratch the word "slut" into it twice with my nail before eventually erasing it with my palm. I don't use soap or brush my teeth. I will not eat or put clothes on. I will not answer the endless ringing phone, change the sheets, or clean the puke next to my bed.

I think about suicide. I think about my boyfriend as the phone rings again. My favorite picture of him shows up for the seventh time as it buzzes on the nightstand. It's him in a pumpkin patch flashing the smile I fell in love with. I push ignore. I'll call him tomorrow. I toss and turn as the sheets writhe around my legs. I close my eyes and try to recount the events.

I was drunk, that was for sure. I wasn't scared until I got into the car. My friend swore he was sober and promised to get me home safe. The windows were down. The air flowed between my fingers. Everything was fine until he pulled into the abandoned parking lot. I thought it was a joke, a parody, something to talk about the next morning over coffee. Was it a weird church he wanted to show me? A statue? An anomaly?

He reached for my neck. I pushed my back against the window. He grabbed both my arms and I froze.

"Do you feel good?" he asked

I flashed back to his apartment moments earlier, my drunken head bobbing with content. His girlfriend had long gone to bed. He pulled out a mirror and a small bag of powder. He said, "You're drunk honey, do one of these. It'll sober you up, it'll make you feel better."

I reached for the straw and nodded in agreement. I had known him for ten years, with no reason to have concern. He pulled out a gun and smiled. My reply was, " I want to go home". We fight in the car. He reminds me he has a gun. He pulls my hair and I scream. He pushes my head down and I punch whatever I can. I break loose. I run. There is nowhere to go. I am drunk. I am high. I am scared.It's so cold. He is screaming my name. I turn around.

I get back into the car. He has his way. I cry.

PART II

I hangout with my friend and her boyfriend exactly two more times, we meet at her house. He smiles at me when she's not looking as if we have a secret nobody else knows. He talks about her friends and that they're all "bitches and sluts" except for me of course, "I'm a good friend," he says with a wink and a laugh.

I tell no one for three months.

When I do, no one believes me.

My boyfriend is the first person I confess to, he says, "You're just saying this to get a reaction out of me."

When I begin to cry he says, "You're lying."

I look down at the ground and wish that I were.

I call my friend, the girlfriend. She asks, "Are you sure that's what happened? Did you really feel in danger?"

My voice trembles with fear and I beg her to listen. She pauses and sighs. It's him, the accused, *her* boyfriend, calling on the other line.

She takes one more breath, I can hear the pity thicken the white noise and says, "It's him, I'll call you right back."

I do not hear from her again.

PART III

Nine months go by. My boyfriend says he "forgives me" but won't look me in the eye. We stop having sex. He sleeps on the couch.

One night a friend comes over. He sits up late with us and drinks. We stumble to the basement and smoke forbidden cigarettes. We talk of dreams and aspirations, movies and books. He takes a long drag off his cigarette and taps it in the ashtray. He stares at the wall and says. " Have you ever heard of (Him, the accused)?

We shift uncomfortably. My boyfriend pulls hard and long on his cigarette as my face distorts with bewilderment.

Our friend is tall and handsome. We wait impatiently to see what he'll say. He kicks the wall. He sways slightly before cracking another beer and says, "He raped two of my friends you know. Gave them some weird drug. Told them it would sober them up then drove them to some parking lot and well, you know…"

I watch my boyfriend turn white. He pushes his hair across his fore-head, a nervous reaction I use to find endearing. He sweats. His body shifts from left to right.

I find myself drunk again. I stand and stumble. My wine glass tilts and a few red drops fall onto my barefoot. I look at our friend then turn to my lover, my confidant, and say, "You can't always believe what you hear."

I slam the door like a child and pretend to revel in victory.

Knowing I will cry myself to sleep, I stomp up the stairs, deciding it is *I* who will sleep on the couch tonight.

10

The Truth (aka) The Fiction

When did my hands start looking so old?

My Fingers had stopped drumming Metallica and were now laid out across the wooden kitchen table, each finger evenly dispersed. Green veins spread across the pale canvas like highway roads on an atlas. My knuckles protruding like white-capped mountains that could potentially break through the epidermis and spew bloody lava all over the oak stained table.

I turn my hands over, disgusted by their tops.

I could have sworn my life lines had been longer, softer, flowing down my wrist, and colliding with my tendon. Instead they look withered, sad, and thirsty. I light a cigarette. The smoke fills my lungs, I pull in more hoping it will coat my eyes, collapse my lungs and send me into a coughing fit, vomit for shock value, because I like shock value.

The smoke escapes my lungs, plunging out of my mouth and nose without so much as a mmhmmh, or ahem.

"Fuck Yes" I say as the smoke releases.

I swear all the time. I swear in my head. I swear in front of my mom, grandfather, father, little brother, at church, on the phone, and in public. (Cock mongrel, fuck fangs, shit balls, ass tooth, cunt breath, are just a few of my favorites.

You would think I was a twelve year-old boy, not a 35 year old woman.

When did my fingers start turning yellow at the tips? Not all of them, just the index and middle fingers of both hands. My boyfriend's fingers are yellow like mine. In the beginning I found it adorable, even admirable.

It reminds me of my old punk rock days. Not giving a fuck. Middle fingers in the air, head half-shaven, rips in my t-shirts strategically placed to not show any nipple, plaid skirts that would tease any dick paying attention, some out of disgust, others out of lust.

I was a fraud. But so was everybody else.

A wave of yellow smoke rolls up my pink nail. Why doesn't soap take the stains out? My mouth tastes like gasoline and an ashtray. If I lit a match would my insides go up in flames? Could I breath a fireball that would engulf the cat-haired-covered curtain in front of me? They both sound pleasant, even relaxing.

After four fucking years of living in this shit hole. I'm still surprised by the ricochet of the refrigerator door on the wooden cupboard, the startling reaction that escapes my lips as the door smacks me on the side and the shock of the future bruise sure to appear on my hip. Why did I open that door in the first place? It was the freezer I wanted. That door bounces off the wall and I catch it before it crashes into my head. The blue bottle is covered in a thin film of frost. The handprint I had placed on the vodka bottle twenty minutes earlier bleeds into the blizzard. I pour the clear liquid until it spills onto the table one drop at a time.

I can't remember when I started drinking vodka straight up. I guess it started in a mixed drink form, vodka cranberries, vodka sodas, vodka martinis, and then vodka with a pickle. Then one day I ran out of pickles.

It can sometimes take a series of gulps to swallow what I like to call liquid Valium. I prefer to go through the motions of this ritual alone simply because of the faces and gagging that can go hand-in-hand with slamming a glass of vodka.

My hands stop shaking as I fill the glass once more. I take my time with the second, I let the liquid coat my mouth and sting my tongue before swallowing. It's the burn I want to feel rolling down my throat and nestling in my stomach.

The clear liquid cauterizing in my stomach suddenly wanted releasing. I run to the bathroom and kneel over the toilet. The purging and the burning felt like a form of masochism that I have accepted. If my boyfriend were here he would have held my hair. Instead a brown lock falls into the toilet, the tip now dripping with stomach acid and vodka.

I don't bother flushing before turning on the shower. I strip my clothes off slowly and piled them behind the door. It was then that I saw me, staring back at me. My eyes are hollow, my cheeks sunken in, my lips cracked with white lines that matched the ones running across my brow. My breasts lay heavy, my nipples no longer pointing upward but down towards the yellow tile beneath my feet.

All these things were me, a person I had known my whole life.

I touch the bruises around my neck again. It had become a ritual over the last few weeks. I wrap my hands around my neck and try to match them up with the two purple, blue, yellow, and green handprints left on it. My thumbs neatly rest on my hyoid bone like his did. In the beginning they looked exactly like what they were, a man's grip on a woman's neck. Time soon manipulated them into blobs of color that bled across my nape. They were not healing as quickly as my wrists. Turtlenecks had now become a staple in my wardrobe.

11

The Hats

She couldn't help herself. The first time was an accident. They had been living together for six months. He had moved into her two-bedroom house, a logical next step of many in their budding relationship. Friends of the couple took turns carrying in boxes of books and clothes, crates of records, and what she use to call "comic books" but was soon corrected by him as "graphic novels". She didn't own much. Never had. Her Croatian mother used to say; "stuff is just stuff". His collections of "stuff" seemed endless. It had taken him six days to unpack and organize. She would come down to the basement after work carrying two Budweiser's and watch with fascination as he pulled each item carefully out of boxes. Everything seemed to have a place. Records were sorted by genres, subgenres, years, then alphabetized, Graphic novels and books got the same treatment. She couldn't help but laugh as he pulled six smaller boxes out of a brown moving box.

"What the fuck are those?"

He pulled out a metal batman lunch box, the lid now propped open so his name written in permanent marker could be seen on the blue plastic handle. He had been placing shoebox after shoebox against the wall like a brick laying pig in a cartoon she recalled watching as a child. He would carefully open each one and examine its insides. When satisfied with the results he would dig into the lunchbox, pull out a Polaroid and tape it to the outside of each shoebox. A date, year, and model number were written on the white space below the posed photographed shoes, one eloquently placed on top of the other. She counted ninety-three boxes of shoes in the newly built wall.

"This is crazy. You know that right? This is something a serial killer would do. You organize your shoes by date? You're like Patrick-fucking-Bateman in *American Psycho.* Is there something you need to tell me?"

He laughed (his perfect laugh, she thought) and grabbed her by her waist tickling her sides until she giggled, spilling her beer on the concrete floor.

Dinner parties took place every other weekend in what was *her's* now *their* small dining room. Friends would comment on how lucky she was and she would look across the room, smile at him, and agree.

It was a year ago that they had met through mutual friends. It wasn't love at first sight, she had never believed in that, but more of a quick breeding fascination. She, of course was immediately attracted to his crooked smile, and the way a piece of his curly brown hair would absently fall into his green eye. After a year and six months her stomach still turned with delight when she would think about him pulling her long red hair as they lay in bed, their first night together, her screaming his name as he buried his face into her neck.

"Have you thought about marriage? When can I expect grandchildren? You're both thirty. Do you know how many kids I had by the time I was thirty?" Would be said to them over Thanksgiving dinners in broken English from her father. They would laugh uncomfortably, holding hands under the table, her mother serving canned fruit as a dessert and calling it a delicacy.

They had always worked opposite hours, him nights at a bar, her days at an ad agency, hence the move.

"At least we'll be able to sleep next to each other all the time," she had said the night she proposed the move. He cupped her face, starring into her brown eyes, and for the first time in their relationship said, "I love you".

The first couple of months were filled with late night dinners on mutual nights off, fucking took place in living rooms, on kitchen tables, and in showers, movies were debated over pillow fights and ass grabs, and talks of getting a dog would take place in the bed at odd times of the night.

She hadn't really spent much thought on the "stuff" in the basement. It was his room now, a happy offering; it was only fair since the second bedroom was now her in-home office. She had been on a cleaning spree, her favorite Beatles album playing in her headphones as her ponytail swept across her neck. She didn't think twice as she descended the basement stairs. The damp rag glided over a lamp he had since childhood, a leather lazy boy he had inherited from his father, a vintage record player given to him by his older brother for his twenty-sixth birthday, and a medium sized metal file cabinet that had taken three of his friends to carry down the stairs.

She pulled the duster from her back pocket and delicately ran it over the library of records, books and Graphic novels. She laughed as she accessed the wall of shoes, admiring their organization. On the opposite wall were seven oak shelves he had built by hand, each exactly fourteen inches apart and held eight baseball caps, evenly spaced. Fifty-six hats was the grand total, she knew without having to count. Each bill was curved. She ran her finger over the shelf and examined the thin gray dust. She lifted a hat up; it was green with a black C on the front, its outline dustless. Maybe it was *Across the Universe* playing on repeat that had distracted her, or the fact that the pattern was not obvious (color coded, or Polaroid carded) that made her think the action would be okay.

She took her left hand and swiped each shelf off, clearing them of all the hats. She sprayed each one with an environmentally safe cleaner and wiped them down until her finger easily glided across them, dust free. She decided to wet a cloth in the kitchen sink and clean each hat, cautiously, not to bend the brim or mar the hats. She then placed them attentively back on the shelves. It wasn't until after dinner, an hour before he was due to be at work that she realized her mistake.

He and his brother had built a shower in the middle of the basement. She had spent two days drinking lemonade and admiring her boyfriend and his brother shirtless, building the shower for "her convenience" in the middle of the room, so when John came home late from work he could shower without disturbing her.

That night she heard the water shut off and pictured him drying off his naked body with his favorite blue towel.

"Sarah!! Sarah, get the fuck down here." His voice traveled up the stairs. The seriousness in his tone was stern enough to make her smile. She had never heard him raise his voice.

"Jesus John, what is it? What happened?" Her lips were stained from the red wine she had drunk during dinner, the glass wobbled as her bare feet planted on the cold concrete floor, a drop spilled onto her pinky toe. He stood shaking. Holding his blue towel tightly around his waist. The brown curl she was so fond of flapped against his forehead.

"What the fuck did you do?"

"What are talking about?"

He pointed at the dustless shelves, his forehead wrinkled with anger, his body still shaking. She started to smirk. She couldn't help it. He looked like an angry wet puppy. She swayed over to him and removed the bouncing curl and kissed his forehead. He pushed her. She fell, her wine glass breaking, the red substance slowly working its way to the drain in the middle of the room.

Sarah kicked herself into the corner farthest away from him. She rubbed her lower back in shock.

"John? What the fuck was that?" They both shook. His towel fell to the floor, his flaccid penis slightly shifting left.

"You touched my shit. Look!" He began to toss hats at her like Frisbees; each one seemed to cut harder and harder into her arms and legs.

"John. Stop it. Please. You're being crazy."

He didn't stop until the last one was tossed into the pile that was Sarah. She didn't move, instead she sat motionless, like a mouse wishing to go undiscovered.

John stood over the thrown hats, then grabbed his towel and went up the stairs.

Sarah didn't cry. She stood up, took off her clothes and sat down on the shower floor. The luke-warm water beat against her back. She wondered if the push would leave a bruise? Sarah rested her chin into her knees and traced the tile floor with her pointer finger, trying to assess the situation. John wasn't a violent person. She knew that's what *all* abused women say. But in this case, it was true. She knew that. He couldn't sit through a *Law and Order* episode without flinching at any sign of distress. He preferred *Pixar* movies to horror films.

She heard the front door slam as she shut off the water. He had taken the only towel, so she walked up the stairs naked, dripping on every step. Sarah didn't go to the bedroom or grab a towel. Instead she went to the kitchen and poured the rest of the red wine into a glass, underestimating how much was left, and deciding not to wipe off the over pour as it bled over the counter.

John was the youngest of three brothers. His father was a drug addict and wasn't around when he was a child. (He would reconnect with him at the age of thirty-four, two-years later, only to have him die of a heart attack, shortly after finding sobriety.) His mother was an attractive woman who kept many suitors throughout the three brothers lives, some wanting to play fathers, others vocally (and physically) showing contempt of their existence. It was a past easily used to excuse future behaviors. The brothers saved these excuses exclusively for tight pinches (cheating, over drinking, and well, now pushing your girlfriend).

Sarah walked to the couch, her nakedness highlighted by a corner lamp and projected out the bay window. She pulled the metal beaded cord of the lamp and waited for her eyes to adjust.

She tried to figure out what emotion she was feeling. Yes, many were consuming her; anger, humiliation, shock, sadness, disbelief, fear, and one that was disturbing her; arousal. Sarah was the youngest of three sisters. Her family had grown up poor. She had fought for everything she had ever wanted. Graduated at the top of her business class, and vowed to herself that she would be making six figures before she was twenty-five (which she succeeded by the time she turned twenty-four). She had always been the one to humiliate (her nickname at work was simply 'the bully' which she knew and secretly loved).

Sarah felt herself getting wet below as her skin was drying above. She rubbed the damp spot between her legs and let out two short moans. Then stopped.

"Jesus Christ." She said aloud

She couldn't bring herself to climax. Her ego too strong to fight a theoretical argument taking place in her head. What a cliché. What a fucking cliché, was repeating, over and over. Of course she was turned on by being humiliated, it was textbook, she thought. Fuck that. Sarah prided herself on her complexity. This was too simple, too easily summed up. She fell asleep to the discussion in her head. She awoke on the couch to John gently shaking her shoulder.

"I'm so sorry Sarah. That will never happen again. Ever. I don't know what came over me. I..."

Tears streamed down his cheeks. She felt them as she pressed her face against his. Sarah accepted his forgiveness. They had make-up sex there, on the maroon scotch-guarded couch and for the first time in their year-plus relationship she did something she had never done before, she faked her orgasm.

Two months went by with a sweet mundane flow. They never brought that night up again. John forgot it. Not even his daily routine of picking out a hat to wear triggered it. Sarah tried. She tried to forget, move on, let the past be (you guessed it) the past. Sometimes it did. Movie and date nights, dinners, work, and day-to-day errands left that night buried in the back of her head.

It was when she was alone, at night, when John would be at work that the hat incident would creep into her frontal lobe and tap. She fell prey to the cliché and freely began masturbating to the violence and humiliation experienced. First in bed, then the couch, slowly making her way down to the shower and eventually doing it in the corner, the corner where he had thrown her.

It was a Friday night. John had left early for work, telling her not to wait up. She had smiled when he kissed her forehead and shrugged off his apology for not having time to do the dishes.

She went down to the corner with a glass of white wine and pulled up her skirt. She didn't bother pulling off her panties; instead she just pushed them to the side. This orgasm came quick, almost anti-climatic; a slight tinge of disappointment and shame overcame her. It was in that spiral she noticed the metal file cabinet towering over her, almost watching her, pitying her. Sarah drank what was left in her glass and stumbled over to it. She pulled on the top handle. Locked. She pulled on the bottom. Same.

She climbed the stairs and then poured another glass of wine. Before taking a sip, she opened a new bottle. She went upstairs and sat on the toilet, her hair falling over her shoulders, her back hunched. She didn't have to pee, but the leftover orgasm had given her a sensation as if she did.

Their bedroom was small. Her dresser was kept in her office. John's next to his hung and ironed t-shirts (color coordinated) in the closet. Sarah dug around in his sock drawer, next his underwear drawer, carefully lifting each folded undergarment. She felt the metal box she had been looking for; Batman staring up at her as if to say, "Congratulations. You did it."

Two small keys lay inside. She held them to the light, grabbed her glass, and the bottle and headed to the basement.

The key slipped in. The top drawer came open with ease. Alphabetical tabs in neon colors stuck above the manila files. Her fingers glided across each one. Phone bills from AT&T were filed under A, bank statements from Wells Fargo under W, Tax forms in the T's, and credit card paperwork under C for Chase, each one stapled and dated. Sarah snickered at her guilt. She grew flush with pride of John's consistency.

She unlocked the second drawer absently, the knot of potential jealousy in her stomach dissipating. It didn't open as smoothly as it's counter part. She had to jiggle it, lift it up and pull to the left before it popped open. Once again she was greeted by color coded, alphabetized tabs.

"What has he decided to organize now?" She said aloud

Sarah sat down on the gray concrete enjoying it's chill under her bare thighs. She finished her drink and poured another. She straddled the metal drawer. She reached for the file labeled K. Sarah couldn't think of anything that started with a K... Yet the file was larger than the others, bulging.

Maybe she had had too much to drink. Maybe the excitement of being a voyeur in her own home had overwhelmed her. Maybe the old saying 'curiosity killed the cat' was true, because as she pulled the file out of the cabinet her hands began to shake. Sarah felt the file begin to slip out of her grip and before she could control it, the file spilled out all over her naked thighs, knocking over the glass of wine. It's contents soaking the innards of the manila casing.

Sarah looked down in horror.

Photographs, Polaroids, and handwritten letters were strewn across her. Each had a date. Each had a name.

Katie, Kim, Kelsey, Kelly, Keira, Kirsten… The dates went back as far as 1995, others dated as early as a week ago. Each girl in different forms of undress, topless, legs spread, in lingerie, handcuffs, some asleep, others wide eyed, and some with his dick posed next to their face. How did she know it was his? Because of the hand holding it. The birthmark conveniently placed between his thumb and pointer finger, a mark he had only recently become comfortable with.

The letters were all addressed to the same PO box and written with similar themes.

"John, last night was amazing. When can I see you again? I'm so wet." Sarah read them aloud. She had trouble focusing and was only able to skim them, the tremble in hers hands causing the words to blur.

Ashley's, Ava's, Beth's, Lucy's, Jackie's… Some girls she recognized as his co-workers or patrons at the bar he worked at, others from shows and local restaurants they liked to frequent on the weekends.

Sarah calmly packed up each file, double-checking to make sure they were properly alphabetized. She crossed herself dramatically the same way she had seen her mother do before certain situations, blessing herself that she had been drinking white wine instead of her usual red. It had dried clear, only slightly warping the envelopes.

She finished the bottle and smoked a cigarette, something she hadn't done in two years.

It was 5:03 am when John got into bed, his weight on the edge awaking her. He climbed in and kissed her neck. She could smell the whiskey on his breath. Sarah kept her eyes tightly shut as he began to snore, a heavy sound he only did when drunk, and that's when she remembered the keys.

She had locked the file cabinet, but in her drunken state had left the keys on the floor. She crept out of bed, tip-toeing like a rebellious teenager about to go on a past curfew adventure. It would be her fourth trip down the basement stairs. Sarah saw the keys. They shined like a dime on a sidewalk in the sun. That's when it happened.

At first it was a cautious act. One she knew was wrong, but couldn't help herself. Sarah pulled out a *Miles Davis* record, careful not to finger-print the black vinyl. She traded its contents with the red collectors edition she found in an *At The Drive In* album. *The Beatles* were soon replaced with *Run DMC, Bob Dylan* now lived in *LL Cool J's* sleeve, and *The Pixies* traded places with *Thelonious Monk*.

A wave of frenzy consumed her. It went on for hours. The wall of shoes were strategically mismatched in their shoebox homes, book jackets unwrapped and rewrapped on anything that would look unsuspicious.

Sarah was sweating by the time she was done. She glanced around the room. It looked untouched. As if nothing had happened.

The only things out of place were the two keys lying next to the file cabinet.

Sarah sat down on the floor for the last time that evening. She unlocked the bottom drawer and pulled out the file labeled S. She found three different photos of Sarah's, none of which were of her.

12

The Nurse

She pinches the pill in her pocket with her pointer finger and thumb rubbing until she can feel the engraved 80 and OC on each side of the tablet. It was a small pill. She'd seen it take down grown men just by entering their stomach.

It wasn't stealing. It was impossible to smuggle anything out of the hospital. In the last months two separate nurses had been caught stealing drugs from patients and were now awaiting trial. One nurse had stolen a man's Fentanyl before he was due to have kidney-stone surgery.

She was quoted in the local paper as saying to the patient, "You're gonna have to man up here." She watched with dilated eyes, clammy palms, sweating forehead, and swaying limbs as the sober patient writhed in agony. The doctor cut an incision into the patients back and inserted a tube down to his kidneys. It took three nurses to hold him down.

Another nurse a few weeks later was caught pretending to be a traveling nurse in several hospitals around the Twin Cities. She would walk in with her scrubs and badge and sneak into rooms with patients on liquid Dilaudid, puncture the IV bag with a syringe and siphon the drug for personal use.

Julie and the other nurses couldn't help but laugh at the stupidity. What Julie was doing wasn't anything like that. It didn't happen often (she liked to tell herself) and she never went out of her way to get pills. Sometimes it just happened; like today for instance.

He was a patient with a chronic back pain. He was an older gentleman who she called Mr. Klein with thinning gray hair. He was sweet, Julie thought, and his wife even sweeter, bringing him a bowl of chicken noodle soup everyday.

It was time to bring him his pain medication and Julie had just started her shift, 3:00 pm to 11:00 pm. She swiped her badge before entering the infirmary and put her fingerprints on the Pyxis machine. She tapped on the touch screen and entered her patients name and the word Oxycotin. The long three-by-three inch metal drawer popped open and she counted the number of blister packs (each containing one green pill in it). She typed in "one" and placed it in her pocket, closing the drawer on her way out.

"How are we feeling today Mr. Klein?" Julie walked towards the patient with a glass of water and carefully ripped open the pack. He had just awoken from his third back surgery, the anesthesia still heavily weighing down his eyes and his breathing pattern showing signs of brief unconsciousness.

"It's time for your pain pill Mr. Klein."

He shook his head at her without speaking then reached for the glass of water. He let the water dampen his lips before swallowing.

"No. No Julie. Not right now. That medication makes me feel nauseous, like I'm going to throw up, and the spins, Julie, the spins make me feel crazy. Sometimes I'd rather have the pain."

She assumed he probably didn't mean what he was saying, honestly wouldn't remember the conversation at all, watching his eyes once again roll back into his head then forward again at her.

"Mr. Klein, why didn't you say something earlier? We could get you something else. I'll talk to the doctor when he comes back around." She cocked her head at him, slipped the pill into her pocket and asked if he needed anything else before leaving the room.

It was now 9:15 pm. He had never asked for the Oxycotin; no one had.

She took two more drags off her cigarette and tossed it in the park, the designated smoking area across from the hospital. A small ash fell onto her blue scrubs and she brushed it off. It left a gray smudge over her breast and a bad smell on her hand. She shoved the hand back in her pocket and caressed the green pill. She would only take half tonight, she decided, just enough to relax with a glass of wine and a movie. Because, she said out loud "I deserve it."

She had graduated top of her class in nursing school. She prided herself on the fact that she could do the New York Times Sunday crossword in twenty minutes flat. A fete few of her friends could boast about. It wasn't that she lacked intelligence; it was more like a self-preservation deficiency that caused her to be in compromising situations. Well that and an unusually low-self esteem. She looked at her watch and lit another cigarette. There was more than enough time to have one more, she'd eat her leftover chicken wings later when she got home, her appetite suppressed by the excitement of the stolen, wait, not stolen, misplaced, better yet, unwanted pill in her pocket.

The *misplacing* of pills started her first year as a nurse at an old folks home. It was two years ago, when she was thirty-three. The senile and their memories or lack of, were easy prey. She never denied them their medication; that would have been unethical.

Handfuls of pills were dispersed to each patient for their blood pressure, arthritis, declining livers, kidneys, brain and nervous systems. Their anxiety and pain all capable of being quelled by a tablet taken twice a day with food, or at least that's what the pharmaceutical reps would state armed with free pens, samples, and pamphlets. A plethora of co-dydramol, morphine, vicodin, oxycodone, klonopin, xanax, and fentanyl would pass through Julie's fingers.

The first time was an accident. The pill had sat untouched in her pocket for weeks. It wasn't until she was doing laundry that she found it tucked in the corner of her scrubs amongst the lint and hair. She always checked her pockets before washing ever since the day she had mistakenly left a lipstick tube in her jeans, ruining the entire load.

She pulled out the white cylinder with an engraved V and tried to remember how it had gotten there. She broke it in half and popped it into her mouth. It was later on that day, laying in her bed, limbs heavy, eyes droopy, mind calm, and body in a degage pose, that she recollected the moment the vicodin serendipitously came home with her.

It was simple. Mrs. Johnson hadn't wanted the pill. She was a seventy-year old woman with mild arthritis, a whippersnapper; one of the few residencies that still received weekly visits from her children and grandchildren.

It was a Monday, that's right, Jules thought as she pushed the half eaten sandwich she had ordered at the peak of her high. The sauce from the steak and cheese had leaked onto her unwashed sheets. She fingered the tin foil it was wrapped in and let it crunch between her nails.

Mrs. Johnson was expecting visitors. It was her grandson's fifth birthday, an age were children still got excited to see grandparents.

"Oh Julie, I'll take all the other medications but I don't want the painkiller, little Davey's coming. I want to remember that moment forever. Those damn Vicodins make me tired. I feel good today, I feel great today!"

Mrs. Johnson stuck out both her hands and flexed them in and out in a pumping motion, to show Julie she was fine. Julie saw the old woman wince once then twice with each pump. Pride and perseverance; she remembered admiring the old lady's strength. She had slipped the pill into her pocket to free her hands. It had been that easy.

Julie hadn't thought about Mrs. Johnson in years. Cancer soon took over the old lady's body. Her pain medication increased. So did Julie's tolerance. She couldn't count how many pills she *misplaced* since then. Truthfully she didn't care. Mrs. Johnson's family had gathered around the hospice bed the day she died. Her grandson Davey sat on the edge his lip quivering. His mother held the old lady's hand and wept silently. Mrs. Johnson took her last breath as her husband stood staring out the window unable to watch.

Julie had stood in the back tapping her clip board almost impatiently wondering what she should have for lunch.

She flicked her final cigarette into the street. It bounced off a pile of snow and rolled under the no smoking sign on the east wall of the hospital. She fingered the pill in her pocket one last time. She had felt nothing that day, the day Mrs. Johnson died, "And that" she whispered out loud, " Is what makes me a great nurse" but this too was a lie.

13

The Bridge

http://www.thesecretroompodcast.com/Episode 147: The Bridge

Top Five Favorites

Music

1. Beatles

2. Paul Simon

3. The Plastic Constellations

4. Lifter Puller

5. Run the Jewels

Albums

1. Lonesome Crowded West

2. Punk in Drublic

3. Half Dead and Dynamite

4. The Predator

5. Pretty Tony

Things I Hate

1. Mayonnaise

2. Yogurt

3. Everyone

4. Everything

5. Me

Ways to Die

1. Cancer

2. Hit by a Bus

3. A fire

4. Possession

5. Old Age

Ways I Think about Dying

1. Jump

2. Pills

3. Gun

4. Sadness

5. Drown